The Babies on the Bus

The Babies on the Bus

Karen Katz

SCHOLASTIC INC.
New York Toronto London Auckland
Sydney Mexico City New Delhi Hong Kong

The wheels on the bus go **round and round**, all through the town.

The doors on the bus

open and **close,**
open and **close,**
open and **close.**

The doors on the bus

open
and
close,

all through the town.

The driver on the bus says,

"Move on back,
move on back,
move on back!"

The driver on the bus says,

"Move
on
back!"

all through the town.

The babies on the bus sing,

"LA-LA-LA!
LA-LA-LA!
LA-LA-LA!"

The babies on the bus sing,

"LA-LA-LA!"

all through the town.

The wipers on the bus go

swish, swish, swish!
Swish, swish, swish!
Swish, swish, swish!

The wipers on the bus go

swish, swish, swish,

all through the town.

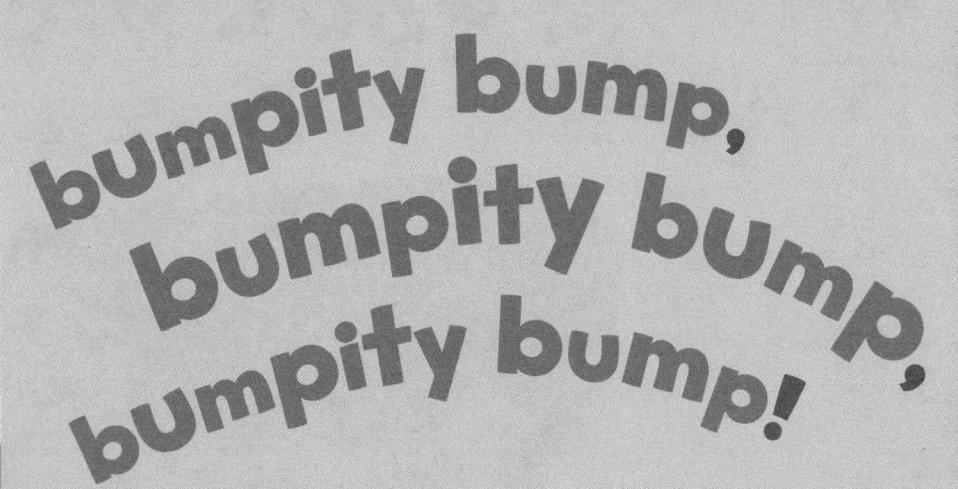

The babies on the bus bounce

bumpity bump,
bumpity bump,
bumpity bump!

The babies on the bus bounce

bumpity
bump,

all through the town.

The horn on the bus goes

Toot, toot, toot!
Toot, toot, toot!
Toot, toot, toot!

The horn on the bus goes
toot, toot, toot,
all through
the town.

"Waah!
Waah! Waah!

Waah!
Waah! Waah!
Waah! Waah! Waah!"

The babies on the bus cry,

The babies on the bus cry,
"Waah! Waah! Waah!"
all through the town.

The driver on the bus says,
"Shush, shush, shush,
shush, shush, shush,
shush, shush, shush."

The driver on the bus says,
"shush, shush, shush,"
all through
the town.

The babies on
the bus fall
fast asleep,
fast asleep,
fast asleep.

The babies on
the bus fall
fast asleep,
all through
the town.

Zoom, Zoom, Zoom,

The motor on the bus goes

Zoom, zoom, zoom! Zoom, zoom, zoom!
Zoom, zoom, zoom!

The motor on the bus goes

all through the town.

The driver on the bus says,

"Everyone up!
Everyone up!
Everyone up!"

The driver on the bus says,

"Everyone up!"

all through the town.

children's museum

The babies on the bus say,
"Bye-bye, bus! Bye-bye, bus!

Bye-bye, bus!"

The babies on the bus say,

"Bye-bye, bus!"

Now it's time to go.

EXIT

For Lena and Gary
and all the bouncing
babies everywhere

ISBN 978-0-545-46909-8

12 11 10 9 8 7 6 5 4 3 2 1   12 13 14 15 16 17/0

Printed in the U.S.A.   08

First Scholastic printing, September 2012

Book designed by April Ward